NEXO KNIGHTS

In a kingdom far, far away, where magic meets technology, live brave knights who are ready to fight anyone who threatens their realm . . . or anyone who tries to steal their food!

MACY

AARON

CLAY

AXL

LANCE

A

B

C

E

D

Take a look at the knights and draw lines to match them with their shields.

JESTRO

This royal jester has just found a magic book in Merlok's library! It will let him unleash monsters! Things aren't going to be all that funny anymore!

Can you spot which monster Jestro wants to release?

> MY FAVORITE MONSTER DOESN'T HAVE ANY HORNS, BUT HE DOES HAVE TWO LEGS, A HOOD, AND AN EYE PATCH.

> GOOD CHOICE!

MERLOK 2.0

LOOK AT THE SCREEN!

A B C D

Merlok used to be a normal wizard—until a big fight with Jestro transformed him into a digital one!

Help his apprentice, Ava, find the right socket and plug him into the extra power supply.

The radar has detected a horde of Globlins nearby, but Robin, an eager knight in training, is too busy untangling a squirebot!

Help fire 3 shells from the cannon by drawing 3 straight lines that go through at least 15 of the monsters.

AARON'S AWESOME DAY!

WOOO HOOOOOOO!

BEING AWESOME MAKES ME SOOOO THIRSTY!

HEY! MONSTER DUDES! GIMME BACK MY SHIELD!

OR RATHER . . . LET ME TAKE IT BACK IN THE MOST AWESOME WAY POSSIBLE!

CAN I BORROW THIS? THANKS!

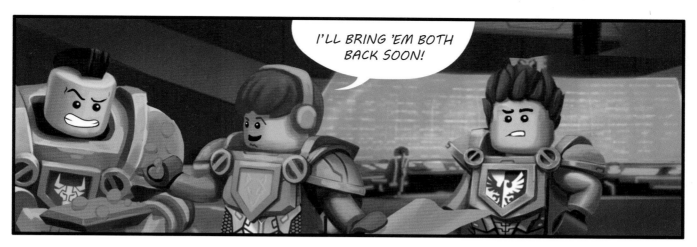

I'LL BRING 'EM BOTH BACK SOON!

WHAT?!!!

WHAT'S WITH AARON? HE TOOK MY KNIGHTS' CODE!

HE TOOK MY SQUIRE-RAZZI!

HE TOOK MY PEAS!

HE TOOK MY FLUFFY PRINCESS DRESS!

HA! SEE YA LATER, SCURRIERS!

OKAY, I GET HOW YOU TURNED THE DRESS INTO A HANG GLIDER, AND MADE A PEASHOOTER WITH MY CODE AND AXL'S DINNER, BUT WHAT'D YOU NEED THE SQUIRE-RAZZI FOR?

TO TAKE SOME TOTALLY AWESOME ACTION PICTURES!

WHATTA KNIGHT!

Introducing the perfect knight . . . Clay! He has Knights' Code running through his veins and all he talks about is armor, arming, and disarming. Isn't he charming?

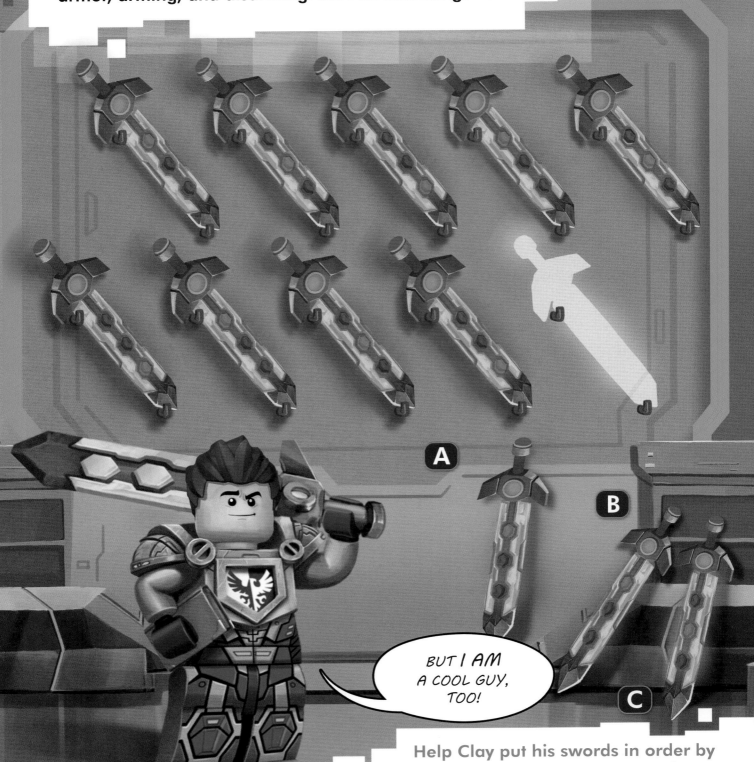

A

B

BUT I AM A COOL GUY, TOO!

C

Help Clay put his swords in order by marking which one completes the pattern at the end of the row.

NEXO POWERS

Cyber magic is very powerful. Merlok uses it to send NEXO Powers to the knights' shields.

Which three of these five shields would form the complete picture of Aaron's shield if combined?

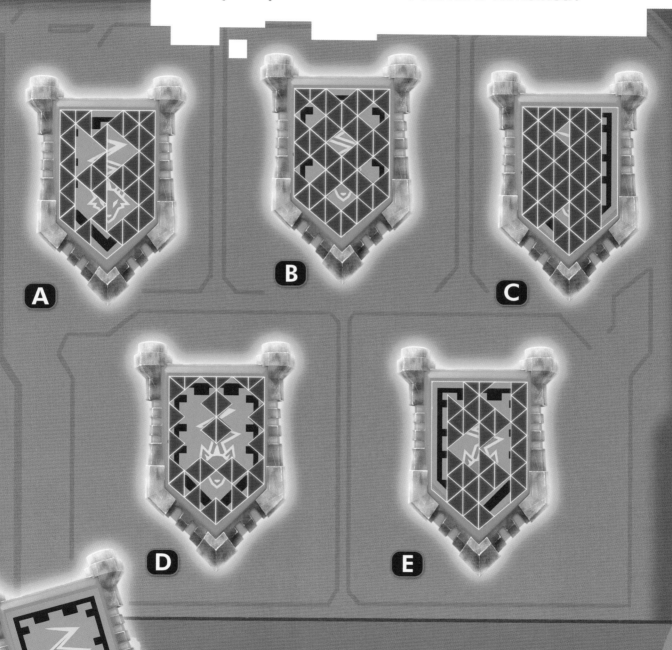

A

B

C

D

E

PICTURE-PERFECT LANCE

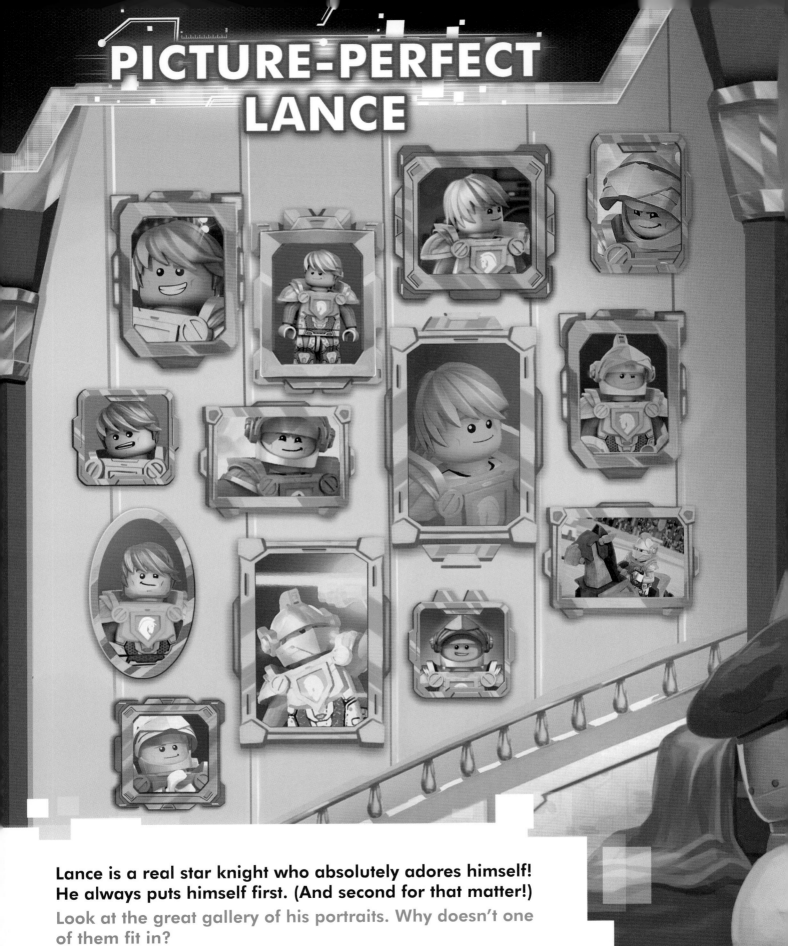

Lance is a real star knight who absolutely adores himself! He always puts himself first. (And second for that matter!)

Look at the great gallery of his portraits. Why doesn't one of them fit in?

Lance's next portrait is being painted right now, but it looks slightly different from the model himself.

Can you spot 8 differences between them?

FORTREX

Lava Monsters, beware! The headquarters of the NEXO Knights is a fortified castle and giant tank all rolled into one! Robin Underwood is a great mechanic, and he takes care of Fortrex.

Help him find the right spare parts for the knights' base.

THE POWER OF TEAMWORK

KA-BOOM! The NEXO Knights' rolling castle, the Fortrex, was under attack by fiery Lava Monsters in the once-peaceful Hamlet of Glockenspiel. Watching nearby, the evil jester Jestro and his partner-in-crime, the vile Book of Monsters, laughed.

"That's it! Tear their little fort apart!" said Jestro with glee.

"They fell right into our trap," said the Book of Monsters. "They're such goody-goodies!"

Brave knight Clay Moorington and fellow NEXO Knights, Lance Richmond, Macy Halbert, Aaron Fox, and Axl (just Axl) were trying to fend off the fiery fiends attacking them.

"These hot little things are ruining my hair!" cried Lance as he batted monster Globlins away.

"These hot little things are everywhere!" added Axl.

"You'd dodge them better if you hadn't had fourteen pork fritters for breakfast," said Aaron.

"We have to work together as a team," Clay called out.

"I hear you, Clay," responded Macy, "but we're being overwhelmed."

How had it come to this? thought Clay. He thought back to when it all begun . . .

Jestro, the king's jester, had stolen Merlok the Magician's magic Book of Monsters. This was a nasty, evil book that contained the most powerful magical monsters from the past. It had been created by Merlok as a sort of "prison" for the nasty creatures it contained. Jestro was going to use it to call forth monsters and take over the realm. Only Merlok's powerful magic saved the day, but Jestro and his new friend, the Book of Monsters, got away . . .

Back at the battle, Clay was wondering how they could beat the monsters. At least they had Merlok back. Only now he was Merlok 2.0, a completely digi-magic form of magician.

"Odds Bodkins, NEXO Knights," cried Merlok 2.0. "Clay is right . . . you must work together to defeat that jerky Jestro!"

The king had given the knights Fortrex, but they still hadn't been fighting as a team for very long. They had to get it together though, or Jestro would destroy Glockenspiel.

"The musical Glockens in this town are in danger," said Clay.

"Don't forget the Spiels," added Aaron. "They're cool, too."

Jestro and the Book of Monsters pressed their attack. While the knights were trying to fend off their Lava Monsters, the devious duo would destroy the Glockenspiel factory in the middle of the town.

"Nobody makes happy music while I'm around," said the Book of Monsters.

Clay realized that they were about to lose, so he did the only thing he could do: he thrust his shield into the air and called on Merlok 2.0 to send them all NEXO Power.

"Merlok! NEXOOOOO Knight!" Clay shouted.

"NEXO Power," Merlok 2.0 responded in a booming voice. "Power of the United Knights!"

ZZZZZZAAAAP! ZZZZZZZING! KA-WOWWEEEEE! With a digi-magic flourish, incredible digi-powers downloaded into each knight's shield.

Clay stepped up and the other knights got behind him. They swung their weapons as if they now contained the power of twenty suns.

"Teamwork, NEXO Knights," intoned Clay, "is the only way to win!"

The NEXO Knights charged towards Jestro and the Book of Monsters, tossing fiery Lava Monsters aside as they did.

Working together, they appeared unstoppable.

"Now what?!" said Jestro, worried.

"Oh, that's easy," said the Book of Monsters. "We . . . RUN AWAY!"

The knights smiled at their victory and struck a heroic pose.

"I love it when we pose heroically like this," said Lance, hoping someone would snap his picture.

"That's what I call getting Glockenspielled," Macy said, grinning.

"No," said Clay, lifting the visor of his helmet. "That's what I call . . . teamwork."

THE WIZARD'S APPRENTICE

Ava has just programmed a digital NEXO game, and Aaron can't wait to try it!

Guide Aaron through the maze to finish the level.

START

FINISH

FIGHTING PRINCESS

Macy is a real princess, but she doesn't actually want to rule Knighton. She prefers fighting ferocious monsters instead!

MACY, YOU PROMISED TO STOP DOING THIS!

SOMEONE HAS TO PROTECT THE KINGDOM . . .

HUNGRY, ANGRY, OR HANGRY?

When always-hungry Axl heads out to fight, all the Globlins hide from the giant knight!

How many hidden Globlins can you spot?

THE BOOK OF . . . HAPPINESS?!

THE FORGOTTEN FOREST

Aaron is fighting Whiparella and her fear-inducing spider-legged minions. These monsters can make their enemies see their worst fears.

YOU'RE THE ONE WITH THE PROBLEM. I'M FEARLESS!

START

Now lead the fearless knight out of this dark forest.

Draw a line from crystal to crystal to reflect Aaron's NEXO Powers and hit all the spiders. Try to hit every one without picking up your pen!

FINISH

BREAKFAST OF CHAMPIONS

Prepare a typical meal for Axl by finding the missing ingredient for each plate:

Plate 1: soup, bread, butter, sausage
Plate 2: noodles, steak, rolls, cheese
Plate 3: 2 chicken legs, 2 lemonade jars
Plate 4: french fries, hamburger, pizza, pancakes
After all that he'll need a 10-minute break.
But then, he'll start getting hungry all over again!

A SQUIREBOT PARTY

The squirebots are having a party. Each bot has an identical friend—except for one!

Find him!

ANSWERS

p. 2

pgs 4–5

pgs 6–7

C

pgs 10–11

B

A **C** **E**

pgs 12–13

pgs 14–15

 5   **2**

1   **4**

 6   **7**

 3

pgs 20–21
Example solution

pgs 22–23

p. 24

D **19**

pgs 26–27

pgs 28–29

1 **D**
2 **B**
3 **A**
4 **C**

pgs 30–31

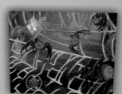